THE PRINCESS AND FROGGIE

THE PRINCESS AND FROGGIE

Stories by Harve and Kaethe Zemach

PICTURES BY MARGOT ZEMACH

A Sunburst Book · Farrar, Straus and Giroux

THE BALL IN THE POND

Once there was a princess.
She had a friend, named Froggie.

One day the princess went
to the park to play ball.

She threw the ball up in the air
and caught it.
She threw the ball up again
and caught it.

She threw the ball up again.
This time she missed.
It fell in the pond.

The princess tried to get the ball out,
but she couldn't reach it.
The ball floated away into the middle of the pond.

The princess ran around to the other side.
She still could not reach the ball.
She almost fell in the water.

The princess started to cry.
She cried and she cried.

Just then, Froggie came.

Froggie said: "What's the matter, Princess?
Why are you crying?"
"My ball fell in the pond," said the princess,
"and I can't get it out."

"Wait a minute," said Froggie.
He jumped into the pond and got the ball.

He gave it to the princess.

"Thank you, Froggie," said the princess.

And she gave Froggie a lollipop.

THE LOST PENNY

Once there was a princess.
One day her mother, the queen, gave her some money
and said: "Go buy apples. Don't lose the change.
Buy yourself a lollipop on the way home."

The princess went and bought the apples.
The man gave her change—one penny.

Then she went to the lollipop shop.
But when she got there
she couldn't find the penny.

It was not in her hand.
It was not in her pocket.
It was not on the floor of the shop.

She sat down and started to cry.
She cried and she cried.

Just then, Froggie came.
"What's the matter, Princess?" said Froggie.
"Why are you crying?"

"I bought some apples and I lost the change.
    And I can't find it anywhere."
"Come with me," said Froggie. He took her hand
    and they walked along the street.

"Look!" said Froggie.

The princess looked, and there was her penny.

She picked it up and said: "Thank you, Froggie.

Come with me to the lollipop shop."

When they got there, the princess said:
"How much are lollipops?"
"Two for a penny," said the lollipop lady.
So the princess bought a green one for herself

and a red one for Froggie.

THE BIRD ON THE KING'S HEAD

Once there was a princess.
Her daddy was the king.
One day a bird came and sat on the king's head.

The king said:
"Princess, please get this bird off my head."

So the princess climbed onto her daddy's lap
and said to the bird:
"Go away, bird. Get off my daddy's head."

The bird flew away.
The princess climbed down.
But then . . .

the bird flew back again onto the king's head.
So the king said:

"Princess! Get this bird off my head!"

The princess climbed back up and said to the bird:
"BAD BIRD! GET OFF THE KING'S HEAD!"

The bird flew away, but . . .

the bird flew back again and sat on her daddy's head.
The king said:

"PRINCESS! GET THIS BIRD OFF MY HEAD
BEFORE I GET ANGRY!"

The princess climbed back up. She said to the bird:
"Bird! You get off my daddy's head!"
The bird flew away and the princess climbed down.
But . . .

as soon as the princess climbed down,
the bird came back on the king's head *again*.
The princess started to cry.
She cried and she cried.

Just then, Froggie came.

Froggie said: "What's the matter, Princess?

Why are you crying?"

The princess said: "Because a bird
is sitting on my daddy's head,
and I can't make him get off."

So Froggie climbed up onto the king's lap,
and he climbed up onto the king's head,
and he *chased* the bird away.

The bird flew away. And it did not come back.
Then the king said to the princess:
"Princess, please get this frog off my head."

So the princess said: "Come down, Froggie."
Froggie climbed down.

The princess thanked him.
The king thanked them both
and gave them each a lollipop.

"If I had one wish, I'd wish for three more."

December 5, 1933—November 2, 1974